THE OAK

by

Geoffrey Patterson

ANDRE DEUTSCH

First published 1979 by
André Deutsch Limited
105 Great Russell Street London WC1

Copyright © 1979 by Geoffrey Patterson
All rights reserved

Printed in Great Britain by
Sackville Press Billericay Ltd

ISBN 0 233 97111 4

First published in the United States of America 1979

Library of Congress Number
79 64263

A long time ago, when very few people lived in
Britain, oak forests covered most of the
countryside. Later, as the population grew, men
needed space to live in and wood to build with.
They cut down the trees to make furniture and
to build houses and ships. They cleared land
for farming.

Although the great forests have gone, many
oak trees still remain. The oak is the biggest of
the trees in Britain, and it lives the longest;
sometimes for as long as four hundred years.
This is the story of one oak tree and the changes
that it has seen.

In 1588 a huge fleet of ships came from Spain to fight against the navy of Elizabeth I. This fleet was called the Armada. Bonfires were lit on the hilltops along the coast to warn people that the Spaniards were coming. But a great storm scattered the Armada. The same wind blew an acorn from a tall oak tree into the grass.

Many years later the acorn had grown into a young tree. Queen Elizabeth was now an old lady. She rested under the oak while out hawking with some of her noblemen. One of her friends had built himself a fine house nearby.

A post mill for grinding corn had been built on the hill. Farmers had settled round about, ploughing and planting the land. They built cottages for their farm labourers.

As the years went by the scattered cottages grew into a village. An inn, *The Magpie*, became the meeting place for the villagers.

In 1665 a terrible illness called the Plague reached the village. It had started in London, and was carried by the fleas that lived on rats. Hardly a family escaped, and nearly every day people were buried. People chalked 'Lord have mercy on us' on their doors to keep the Plague away. When it came, they had to put a red cross on the door as a warning. Work on the new church had to stop as there was no one left to carry stone or mix mortar.

In those days punishment was quick and hard. If you were caught lying or stealing you were put in the stocks. A tramp would be branded on the ear with a hot iron and then whipped from the village.

One day the innkeeper of *The Magpie* was caught selling bad ale. His punishment was to be locked up in the stocks near the oak tree. People threw bad eggs and rotten vegetables at him. Even his poor wife was not allowed to help him.

Life was very hard, but people did manage to enjoy themselves . . .

G. OAKLEY

FOR SELLING
BAD ALE!
AT THE MAGPIE INN
JUNE 7, 1700

SOAP WATER

. . . especially on May day, when the villagers set up a
Maypole on the green to celebrate the coming of summer.
A table under the oak was filled with good things to eat.
They carried ale from *The Magpie* in great pitchers. Dancing
to the music of the fiddle and drum went on late into the

night. Each village had its celebrations because few people travelled on the rough and dangerous roads.

In 1750, though, a preacher braved the bad roads and arrived in the village . . .

. . . His name was John Wesley. He travelled on horseback all over England preaching in the open because he thought the services in the churches were too difficult for ordinary people to understand. The village parson did not like John Wesley at all, because he took away his congregation. But Wesley did not mind. He knew the people who came to listen to him, came because they wanted to.

By 1830 the village had grown into a town. It was important enough for the stage coach to come twice a week. A toll-gate was built at the entrance to the town, and people had to pay a toll to enter. This money was used to repair the road. The coachman had to pay one shilling before he could pass through. All horsemen had to pay, and even the shepherd had to pay twopence to drive twenty sheep to market. Once a rider jumped the gate. The townspeople thought he was a highwayman, so they fixed long spikes to the top of the gate to stop people jumping over it.

In 1840 *The Magpie* was pulled down and Mr Griffin built a store where it had stood. Every year the summer fair was set up on the oak tree green in the centre of the town. People came from miles around to watch and join in the fun.

Most of the other oak trees in the neighbourhood had been cut down. The wood was used to build more houses or repair old ones. But the townsfolk had grown fond of the oak on the green. They couldn't imagine the town square without it.

Everything that was important to the town took place in the square. When there was a big meeting, a special platform called a 'husting' would be set up. People made speeches on the husting to persuade the townspeople to vote for them in an election. Sometimes the meetings were very rowdy; because they gave people their only chance to say what they thought about new laws. Children climbed the oak tree to watch the fun.

After 1850 the town began to grow very fast. Mr Griffin's store, which had sold seed and corn for so long was pulled down. Mr Silas Hart, a manufacturer, put a factory in its place. The factory made steam engines, and many people worked there for very long hours every day. Smoke poured from the tall chimneys. Soon the oak tree was black with soot. Some of its branches died.

The roads had to be widened to carry the huge carts taking goods in and out of the factory. The town square became very small.

The oak tree was now nearly three hundred years old. That winter there was a terrible storm. It blew tiles from the factory roof. It blew down dead branches from the oak tree, and workers from the factory gathered the wood for fires.

One summer's day in 1880 something very important happened. The railway came to town. For months men had been laying rails and building a station. Now the first train steamed in. Everyone turned out to see it. For the first time the goods made in Mr Hart's factory and all the other factories could be sent by train over the whole country. People who could afford it travelled on the trains to visit friends, or go away for holidays.

The big house that had been built for one of Queen Elizabeth's friends was now nearly in the middle of the town. A rich factory owner and his family lived in it. The post mill on the hill, and the oak were the oldest things left in this busy growing town.

In 1914 war was declared against Germany. A large tent was put up on the green to recruit soldiers to fight. Men came from miles around to join the army. Many of them thought that fighting would be a great adventure. But the war was a long and terrible one. Many soldiers were killed, and others badly wounded. While the men were away fighting, the women worked in factories making guns and shells.

By 1952 nothing was left of the original village, or even of the Victorian town except the church and the oak. The oak was almost four hundred years old, and almost dead. Its one surviving branch was held up by supports.

Life in the town was more comfortable than it had ever been. Mr Hart's factory had been replaced by a cinema. People drove their own cars or rode in large buses. Roads were wider and had smooth tar surfaces.

At last the old oak died. At first no one noticed that its branch had no leaves. Then someone realised how lucky they had been to have a tree in the middle of their town.

So the council planned a special ceremony, and the mayor and his wife planted a new oak sapling. As he patted the earth firmly down on the roots he said, 'What changes, I wonder, will this new tree see in the next four hundred years.'